DORY
FaNTaSMaGory

ABBY HANLON

ff

FABER & FABE

For Ann Tobias, my fairy godmother

First published by Dial Books | Penguin Group (USA) LLC
375 Hudson Street | New York, New York 10014
A Penguin Random House Company
Copyright © 2014 by Abby Hanlon

This UK edition first published in 2017
by Faber and Faber Limited
Bloomsbury House, 74–77 Great Russell Street,
London WC1B 3DA

Designed by Jennifer Kelly

The right of Abby Hanlon to be identified as author
of this work has been asserted in accordance with Section 77
of the Copyright, Designs and Patents Act 1988

A CIP record for this book
is available from the British Library

ISBN 978–0–571–32558–0

2 4 6 8 10 9 7 5 3 1

Printed by CPI Group (UK) Ltd, Croydon CR0 4YY

FANTASMAGORY

a dream-like state where real life
and imagination are blurred together

CHAPTER 1
Such a Baby

My name is Dory, but everyone calls me Rascal.
This is my family. I am the little one.

My sister's name is Violet and my brother's name is Luke. Violet is the oldest. Violet and Luke never want to play with me. They say I'm a baby.

"Mum! Rascal is bothering us!"

"What is she doing?" calls my mother.

All summer long, whenever I try to play with Luke and Violet, they say, "PLEASE LEAVE

US ALONE!" Well, I'm not going to leave. But I can't think of what to say, so I ask questions. Any question I can think of.

"I can't wait for school to start so we can get a break from Rascal!" says Violet.

"Me too!" grumbles Luke.

"Don't talk about school!" I cover my ears. I never want summer to end. I like to stay at home in my nightgown instead of getting dressed for school.

"It's a winter nightgown," says Violet.

"And it's inside out," says Luke.

"And it's backwards," says Violet.

"So what?" I say.

"So, now that you've turned six, you need to stop acting like such a baby!"

"Why do you always call me a baby?" I complain.

"Because you talk to yourself," says Violet.

"And you have temper tantrums," says Luke.

"And you play with monsters," says Violet.

Talk to myself? I have no idea what they are talking about. I never talk to MYSELF. I talk to my friend Mary. No one can see her except me.

MARY, it's lunch time!!

Mary *always* wants to play with me. She thinks I'm the greatest.

At night, Mary sleeps under my bed.

During the day, Mary follows me around. She wants to do whatever I'm doing. I usually don't mind, but sometimes I have to tell her no.

"Okay. Mary, what do you want to play?" I ask.

Here are some things Mary likes to do:

Try and steal Violet's doll, Cherry

fake sleep

Sneak cookies from
the high cupboard

exercise club

Get dragged around the house in a laundry basket

Look for Monsters

The Toilet Monster   The Ketchup Monster   The Vacuum Monster

Mary is my favourite, but my house is actually full of monsters. There is the Toilet Monster, who comes into the bathroom if you sit on the toilet for too long.

There is the Ketchup Monster, who makes weird noises when you squeeze the ketchup.

There is also the Laundry Monster,

The Laundry Monster

The Living Room
Monster

The Broken Drawer
Monster

the Broken Drawer Monster, the Vacuum
Monster, the Upstairs Hallway
Monster, the Living
Room Monster,
and more.

Upstairs
Hallway
Monster

I try to warn Luke and Violet when I see one.

"Watch out! It's behind you!"

"AHHH! There's a monster in your underwear!"

"RUN! THE VACUUM MONSTER IS COMING!"

But Luke and Violet don't appreciate it.

After dinner Violet and Luke say they have something important to tell me.

I follow them upstairs, skipping steps. I'm so excited. What can it be? Violet lets me sit on her bed. Maybe she will let me play with Cherry.

Very slowly Violet asks me, "Rascal, have you ever heard . . . of . . . someone named Mrs Gobble Gracker?"

I shake my head no.

"Well, Mrs Gobble Gracker is a robber, and she steals baby girls," says Violet.

"And she is five hundred and seven years old and has very sharp teeth!" adds Luke.

"And, well," says Violet, "you're going to be really surprised when I tell you this."

"What?" I say. I am dying to know.

"She's been looking for you," Violet says quickly.

"Are you serious?" I ask.

"Dead serious," she says.

"Mrs Gobble Gracker is looking for *me*?" I ask in amazement.

"Shhhh," says Luke. "She's so scary you have to whisper when you say her name, like this: *Mrs Gobble Gracker* . . ."

"So, if I were you, I would stop acting like such a baby . . . so she doesn't come and get you," says Violet. For a moment, I'm quiet.

This is a lot to think about. Luke and Violet stare at me, as if they are waiting for me to cry. "How will she get in the house? Does she come

in the front door? Will she ring the doorbell?"
I ask them.

Before they answer, I have some more questions, "Is she sneaky? Will I have to battle her? Does she wear a long black cape? Is it made out of fur? Is it real fur or fake fur? Are her teeth rotting? Does she brush them? Does she have a really creepy-looking nose? Does she have a cat? Does she live in a cave? Does she have really long bones?"

"WE DON'T KNOW! LEAVE US ALONE!" they shout, shaking their heads and walking away fast.

I follow Luke and Violet around the house.

"Oh my gosh! What have we done?" says Luke, covering his ears.

Is she a vegetarian?

Does she vote?

Is she nocturnal?

Does she like ice cream?

Does she like anything?

Is she powerful?

Does she have a mobile phone?

DOES SHE EAT RUBBER CHICKENS?

"This is the worst idea we have ever had," says Violet, trying to get away from me.

"Ever," says Luke. "Ever. Ever. Ever."

"I don't even want to know what happens next," says Violet.

CHAPTER 2
"Did You Hear the Doorbell Ring?"

The next morning I warn Mary. "Mrs Gobble Gracker is five hundred and seven years old, and she has black teeth that are sharp like needles, and her pockets are full of dirty tissues. And . . . she could be on her way over here right now, so don't act like a baby."

I've never seen a monster so scared.

Too tight.

When I hear
the doorbell, I run
downstairs.

"Okay! I'll get it," I say.

I run and hide under my parents' bed. There's something warm and furry under the bed. Someone is already hiding under this bed. It's Mary.

"Have you seen my cape?" I whisper. Mary reaches behind her and hands me my cape, all wrinkled up in a ball. She *always* takes my things and doesn't return them.

"I'm going to battle," I tell her as I put on my cape.

"Can I help?"

Nope. Too dangerous.

Then, as fast as I can, I run into Luke's room to look for his darts. But when I hear footsteps coming closer, I dive into his closet to hide.

It's dark and warm and sort of smelly.
Actually, I'm very happy in the closet, so I
decide to stay. Days and days go by, probably.
I can hear my family saying, "Where's Rascal?"

"Heee, heee! They'll never find me!" I giggle.

The footsteps again! OH NO! SHE'S
GOING TO FIND ME!

The closet door opens.

It's just boring old Luke!

"Rascal, what on earth are you doing in here?" he asks me.

"LEAVE ME ALONE!" I scream. I am so angry that he ruined my hiding spot.

"DON'T FIND ME. DON'T FIND ME!" I shout.

Then I kick and bang and throw some things. I cry so hard that the room looks blurry and upside down.

After I've finished
crying, I feel much
better. "Can I borrow
a dart?" I ask Luke,
drying my tears.

"You're nuts," he says, and walks away,
which I think means yes.

I take the dart and run. In the hallway, I run
into Mary. She is pointing and jumping up and
down. "Mrs Gobble Gracker went downstairs!
She's in the living room! What are you going
to do?" she yells.

"I'm going to shoot her with this special
sleeping dart. It will make her sleep for a
hundred years."

"Wow!" says Mary. "That's a good idea."

"Don't follow me," I warn her.

There she is! Just sitting there! I hold my dart ready to shoot it across the room. Ready, one, two … Wait a minute. What did Violet just say?

"I'm the mummy and
you are the daddy," says Violet.

Are they playing house? I stop my battle.
I drop my dart. I want to play house.

"Now, we just need a baby," says Violet.

Baby???? Did somebody say baby????

My sister and brother look at me very carefully, trying to decide. I show them my cutest baby face. "Goo," I say.

"Hhhhmmmm," says Luke.

"Wellllll . . ." says Violet.

"Hummmm," says Luke.

"I have a better idea!" says Violet, grabbing Cherry. "Cherry can be the baby!"

"Great idea," says Luke. "She's much quieter."

"And cuter," says Violet.

Stupid old baby Cherry, I think. Using my scariest voice, I clench my teeth and warn her, "Just wait, one day I'll get you."

As I walk away, I hold my head up high and think, I don't have time to play anyway. I'm *far* too busy.

But what *was* I so busy doing? I can't remember.

banana
peel

I know I was in the middle of something . . .

When I get back to my room, I snuggle in bed with my bunny. Then Mary comes in with my dart.

"Oh, yeah!" I say, "I was just about to shoot Mrs . . . Uhhh . . . sshh . . . did you hear that?" Creaky sounds are coming from the stairs. Even the Upstairs Hallway Monster is scared and wants to hide out in my room. We peek out and see Mrs Gobble Gracker looking angrier than before. It's time for me to be the brave one.

"Three, two, one . . ." I whisper.

And then I jump out and shoot my dart.

Mrs Gobble Gracker stumbles around. She is walking into the wall, her knees are bending, her eyes are closing . . . she collapses! "I'll find that girl when I wake up," she mumbles, and then she is sound asleep.

I have to tell Luke and Violet! They should know that I shot Mrs Gobble Gracker, because I was so quick and tricky and I had such good aim. They should know that no baby could do what I did. They should know!

I run to the living room and jump right on Violet's lap. I cup my hands around her ear.

I whisper my secret. "Mrs Gobble Gracker is asleep in the upstairs hallway! I shot her with a sleeping dart! I'm dead serious."

"Mum! Rascal is bothering us!" calls Violet, pushing me off her lap.

"What is she doing?" calls my mother from the kitchen.

"She's spitting in my ear!"

"No, I'm not! I'm telling you a secret!" I shout.

But before my mother comes in the room, I run away as fast as I can. As I'm dashing up the stairs I hear my mum say, "Where did Rascal come up with this crazy Mrs Gobble Gracker game?"

I stop to listen.

"I have no idea," says Violet.

"How would *we* know?" says Luke.

Then I run down the hallway to my room, being careful not to trip on the body lying on the floor.

CHAPTER 3
Chickenbone

As I step over Mrs Gobble Gracker's body on my way to breakfast, I start to worry. One hundred years *sounds* like a very long time, but what if one hundred years goes by really fast? I decide to wear my cow costume as a disguise just in case Mrs Gobble Gracker wakes up. Just to be safe.

"Aren't you hot in that?" asks Luke.

"No. Yes. I don't want Mrs Gobble Gracker to recognise me."

"Stop talking about Mrs Gobble Gracker!" screams Violet.

"Stop talking about Mrs Gobble Gracker!" I copy her.

While Mrs Gobble Gracker is asleep, I finally have time to hang out with Luke and Violet.

I try and get Luke and Violet to laugh at me. Cereal time, I've discovered, is the best time for laughing. If I can get milk to come out of my nose, they always laugh. And if my parents sleep late, I can make them laugh by saying bathroom words.

But after cereal time, I have to work much harder to get their attention.

"If you want, you can milk me," I offer Violet.

"Eurgh," says Violet.

"Okay, I'll milk myself and fill up a glass for you," I offer.

"GET AWAY FROM ME!" screams Violet.

I follow Luke and Violet around the house and think of ways to impress them. Mary follows me.

"Can I draw a moustache on Mrs Gobble Gracker while she is asleep?" asks Mary.

"No, that is far too risky!" I tell her.

"But she's snoring really loudly!" says Mary.

"I'm busy," I say, waving her away.

"Hey, guys, do you want to see a magic trick?
See the stick in this hand?" I say. Then I put my
hands behind my back.

"Now it's in this
hand. Ta-da!!"

"That's the worst trick
I've ever seen," says Luke.

They didn't even want to see me eat a napkin.

"Hey, guys, did you know that I can sing without opening my mouth? I'm dead serious. Listen!"

"Can you please hum somewhere else?" says Luke.

"It's not humming, it's singing!" I say.

"Wait a minute . . . is that sweat?" says Violet, looking up. "Are you covered in sweat?" she asks. "Take that thing off!"

"Nope." I say, and fold my arms. "I will not."

"Why do you always have to act like such a baby?" asks Violet.

Then my mum yells:

RASCAL, it's a hundred degrees. Take that costume off right this second!!

I am boiling mad! "I was singing! You are interrupting!" I collapse onto the kitchen floor. The tile feels cool on my hot face. My tears fall onto the diamond patterns in the tile that I know so well from so many temper tantrums on the kitchen floor. As I'm screaming and kicking and crying, I unbutton my cow costume and strip down to my underwear because *it's far too hot to have this temper tantrum in a cow costume* . . . **not** because they told me to!

64

When I'm
finished, I put
my swimming
costume on
and go outside.

I find Mary asleep under a tree.

"Are you real sleeping or fake sleeping?" I ask her.

"Real sleeping," she says without opening her eyes. Now even Mary doesn't want to play.

I lie in the hammock all by myself and think maybe Luke and Violet are right. Maybe I am a baby. I think of all the babyish things I do: I still smell my bunny and suck my fingers to fall asleep. I still put my clothes on inside out. I still can't whistle. I still overflow everything I pour. I still want to wear my nightgown all day.

When I look up at the trees through my tears, I see someone up there looking down at me.

"Who are you?" I ask, rubbing my eyes, squinting into the sun.

"I'm your fairy godmother," says a little man, crawling down from the tree like a koala.

"Are you sure?" I ask. "You don't look like a fairy godmother."

"Well, pretty sure," he says, but he looks sort of confused to me. "Well, the important thing is, I'm here to help you." He says his name is Mr Nuggy and that he lives in the woods.

"Great, I really need help!" I say. "Can you turn me into something else? I have too many problems as a human."

"Sure," he says. "How about a pineapple?"

"Ummm. Okay," I say, shrugging. "Why not?"

He takes out his wand, "One! Two! Three! TA-DA!"

I look down at my body. "I don't feel like a pineapple," I say. "Do I look like one?"

Mr Nuggy looks at me very carefully. He sniffs me. And pokes me. Then sadly he shakes his head no.

But then I have an idea. "How about a puppy?" I say. "Can you turn me into a puppy?"

"Definitely," he says, jumping up excitedly. "No problem at all!" He's lucky that I'm already really good at turning into a puppy.

"One, two, three." He waves his wand. I drop to my hands and knees.

"*Woof, woof, woof,*" I bark and wag my tail. Mr Nuggy looks very pleased.

I turn into a puppy just in time . . .

"Where did that little girl go? She was just out here. And where did this stupid dog come from?" Mrs Gobble Gracker asks Mr Nuggy.

"You must be imagining things," says Mr Nuggy. "There's no girl here."

"I know you're up to something, Nuggy," she says. "Your silly little tricks have never worked on me."

"Watch out," says Mr Nuggy. "This dog bites."

I bark my head off at Mrs Gobble Gracker.

"Somebody get this dog to shut up!" says Mrs Gobble Gracker. She has absolutely no idea it's me!

Rrr-UFF!

"Woof, woof!" I say, which means, "My human days are over." And I really mean it.

Mr Nuggy says, "I have to go now. My wife needs me home for dinner." He starts to climb back up the same tree.

"Woof, woof, woof," I bark up the tree after him, which means, "Wait! What's your phone number?"

"You can call me from any banana," he calls down. "No numbers."

Then he disappears into the summer leaves.

Violet and Luke come outside to play Frisbee, and I run to tell them the news.

"I have great news! Mrs Gobble Gracker will never find me."

"Really? You decided to stop acting like a baby?" asks Violet.

"No, I decided to stop acting like a human," I say.

"Oh for goodness' sake," says Violet. "Don't tell me. I don't want to know."

"No problem," I say, "because I can't talk anyway. *Woof, woof. Woof, woofy, woof, woof,*" I say, chasing after the Frisbee.

"Go away," says Violet.

But Luke says, "Come here, puppy." And he pats me. "What's your name, puppy?"

I have to think of a VERY good name, so that Luke will be excited to play with me. I concentrate really hard.

Finally . . .

I say my name without really opening my mouth because puppies don't talk: "Chickenbone."

"Your name is *Chickenbone*?"

I nod my head yes and say, *"Woof, woof, woof."*

Luke looks pleased.

"Do you have an owner?" he asks.

I shake my head no, and make my saddest puppy eyes ever.

"Well," he says, patting me, "I could be your owner. But you have to be a good dog."

"Woof, woof, woof!!" I jump around and wag my tail and do somersaults to show how happy I am.

It turns out that Luke really wants to be a dog owner. I never knew.

I have long shaggy white fur with brown

spots, and I have a pink polka-dotted bow, and a wet nose, and I'm very jumpy and I usually have drool on my face. Luke just can't get enough of me. He *loves* Chickenbone.

And that's how I became a dog named Chickenbone, and how Mrs Gobble Gracker was left hanging around my house looking sort of bored and confused. I suppose she is waiting for me to come back.

CHAPTER 4
If You Take a Dog to the Doctor

Luke puts my cereal bowl on the floor for me, and I hungrily eat it up. He gives me treats (which is more cereal) when I do my tricks. Here are my tricks:

lie down

spin

sit

Then I chase my dad
down the sidewalk as he
leaves for work.

"*Woof, woof!*" I say, and jump on Violet, who
is still trying to get used to me. "Stop licking
me!!" she screams. "Yuck!! Help!! Rascal is
licking me again!!!"

"Rascal, put
your tongue back
in your mouth!"
yells my mum.

At breakfast, I pick up socks with my mouth and bring them to my owner. I make my little puppy begging sounds until he throws the sock for me to fetch.

"I've got to go. Be a good little dog today," my owner says. I lie on my back so he can pat my belly. Luke and Violet are going to their friend's house. If I weren't a dog, I'd be really jealous.

Instead I'm so happy that I get to stay home all day and chew on socks with Mary.

But my mum surprises me with some terrible news: I have to get dressed.

"Put these on," says my mum, grabbing the socks from my mouth.

"Woof, woof," I say, which means no.

"Rascal! We have to go! I'm not kidding!" she says. "You have an appointment at the doctor today. You have to have a checkup before you go back to school."

"Woof, woof," I tell her, and shake my head no. I don't want to get dressed because I don't want to go anywhere. I want to stay at home in my nightgown, which is actually part of my fur. "NOW!!!" yells my mum.

"Dogs don't get dressed. *Woof!*"

My mum says, "We are in a huge rush, let's go!" But no matter how many times she says it . . . *"Dory, did you hear me say we are in a rush?? We have an appointment. We can't be late . . . "* it just doesn't mean anything to me, *because I'm a dog!*

"A woof-woof-woof-woof, woof . . . woof . . . a woof . . . woof, woof, woof," I say, which means: "No thank you. I'm just going to stay at home and chew on socks."

We are already on the pavement by the time
my mum finally gets my dress over my head.

I cry and have a huge fit, and people walk by
and stare at us.

I had planned on changing back into a girl when we got to the doctor's office. But I discovered it became impossible to change out of being a dog. I was stuck as a dog and there was nothing I could do about it. These things just happen to me.

The doctor is very smiley. She asks me lots of questions.

"How old are you, Dory?"

"*Woof, woof!*" I say.

"What grade are you starting?"

"*Woof!*"

"Dory, you need to answer the doctor," says my mum, who looks embarrassed.

"I see you like to pretend you are a puppy. You are a very cute puppy," says the doctor. "What else do you like to do?"

"*Woof, woof, woof!*" I say.

"I'm so sorry," says my mum. "Dory is very imaginative, a little too imaginative."

"Wonderful," says the doctor, and she pats me. I want to lick her.

My mum whispers to me, "Put your tongue back in your mouth."

The doctor listens to my heartbeat, looks inside my ears, takes my blood pressure and my temperature, and makes my knees jump, and I am a good little puppy for all of it.

Then the doctor says she needs to check my eyes. She asks me to look at a chart, cover one eye, and say what letter she is pointing to. She points to an *E*.

"*Woof?*" I say.

My mum whispers, "Dory, if you don't say
the letters, she's going to think you can't see
them, and you are going to have to get glasses.
So you need to speak."

I imagine myself
wearing glasses and
it's very cute.

"What letter is this?"
asks the doctor pointing to an *F*.

"*Woof?*" I say.

My mum says, "I'm so sorry.
I know Dory can see perfectly
well. Maybe we'll have to do
this another day."

"Okay," says the doctor. "No problem. There's
just one more thing we need to do."

And right when I least expect it, just as the
doctor is saying what a *very healthy little puppy I
am* . . . she is holding a needle. I try to get away,
but I'm not fast enough. OOOOWWWW!!!!
I scream and cry.

1 Least expect it.

2 What's this?

3 Oh no!

4 Aaahhh!

5 Lollipops?

Then the doctor holds a basket of lollipops in front of me. "You can choose one lollipop for now, and one for later," says the doctor, smiling. My tears crawl straight back into my eyes when I see that basket of lollipops. I choose one yellow lollipop for now, and just when the doctor least expects it, I poke the lollipop stick right in the doctor's thigh!!!

"Ouch!" she says.

"That's an injection for you, too," I say.

"So you *can* talk," she says, smiling.

And then I make my angry puppy face, and growl. *"Gggrrr,"* I say, showing her my pointy teeth.

When it's time to go home, my mum puts my yellow lollipop in her purse and I know it's gone forever. I quickly put my shoes back on. My mum doesn't even have to ask me because I can tell by the way she is breathing that I should just do it.

On the way home, we pick up Luke and Violet at their friend's house. I quietly whimper like a dog to Luke so my mum can't hear. I raise my paws and make my eyes look droopy.

But my mum hears everything. *"Dory, that's it! I'm finished! No more dog today!"* she snaps at me from the front seat.

I pout.

And for a few minutes, it's quiet in the car.

And then I whisper, "Who wants to hear how loud I can hum?"

CHAPTER 5
Time-out

When we get home from the doctor, I am in huge trouble. My mum tells me I have to go to my room for time-out. I say, "You can just leave my dog food in a bowl outside my door, *woof*!" This makes my mum so angry that she grabs my paw and drags me up the stairs.

"Walk!" she says.

"I am!" I cry.

"On two legs!!!" my mum yells.

Alone in my room, I suddenly don't feel like being a dog at all. I've got too many problems as a dog. I show Mary my wound. She feels very bad for me.

I put my nightgown back on and then I open my bedroom door a tiny bit. I can hear my family talking about me in the kitchen.

"Rascal gave the doctor an injection!" Luke says, laughing.

"She is out of control!" Violet says. She is laughing, too.

Then I hear an unfamiliar voice. "And she still got a lollipop?" says the voice. Who was that? It sounded like a wicked old . . . huuuuuuuh?!! Was that Mrs Gobble Gracker? I do not believe it. I walk closer to the stairs to hear better.

"All she could do was bark. I've never been so embarrassed in my life!" says my mum.

"How babyish!" laughs the voice. Now I'm sure; it *is* Mrs Gobble Gracker. Are they all sitting around the kitchen table together? And laughing at me? And it sounds like they're eating popcorn!

"Time-out is just what she needs," says my mum.

"I agree. Keep her locked up," grumbles Mrs Gobble Gracker with her mouth full of popcorn.

I run back to my room to tell Mary. "Mrs Gobble Gracker is downstairs *eating popcorn* with my family. *POPCORN!*"

"What's the big deal about popcorn?" asks Mary.

"She is eating popcorn with *my* family!" If Mary doesn't understand, I can't explain it!

"What are you going to do?" asks Mary.

"No more hiding! No more disguises! No more tricks!" I yell. "Something serious has to be done!"

"Like what?" she says.

"Give me that banana. I'm calling Mr Nuggy!"

"Hello? Hi, it's me. Mrs Gobble Gracker is eating popcorn with my family. Yes, I said popcorn . . . I can't believe it either, so can you please come back?"

Wow, that was fast.

Mr Nuggy crawls in the window and wipes his muddy boots.

"I've brought ingredients for a poison soup," he says. "This is how we get rid of Mrs Gobble Gracker . . . permanently."

"What will happen when she eats the soup?" I ask.

"Well, first she will choke a little bit, and then feathers will come out of her ears, and then her eyeballs will turn into gloppy yogurt, and then she'll drop dead."

"Oh!" I say, hugging him. "You are the best fairy godmother in the world!"

But, something isn't quite right.

"I don't mean to be picky," I say, "but could you try and look *a little* bit more like a fairy godmother?"

"What do you have in my mind?" he asks.

I run to my closet to get some dress-up clothes.

Perfect.

Next, we make signs for the door because Mr Nuggy says we need privacy to make our soup.

After we hang up the signs, there's a knock on the door.

It's Luke. "Mum said you can come out of time-out now."

"No thanks," I say, and shut the door. Time-out is turning out to be *far* too much fun.

We don't want any more interruptions so we decide to send Mary out to be our spy. "Tell us if she's coming. And wear this wig!" I say, and give her a push out the door.

Now that it's quiet, Mr Nuggy and I finally start cooking. We make the deadliest, most delicious poison soup for Mrs Gobble Gracker's dinner.

Ingredients

black olives

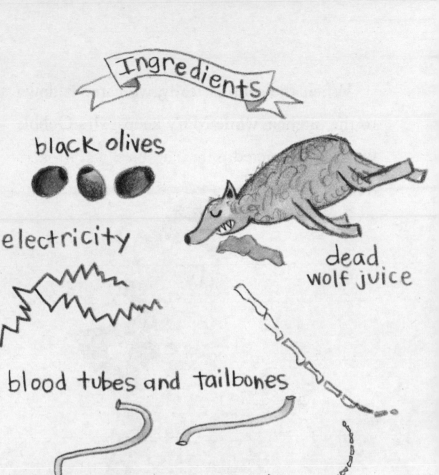

electricity

dead
wolf juice

blood tubes and tailbones

l the rotten parts of all
he apples in the world

and of
course
chicken
broth

BROTH

When the soup is ready, we carry it down to the kitchen, while Mary keeps Mrs Gobble Gracker distracted.

Then Mr Nuggy and I gather materials for a giant fort where we can hide until dinnertime, while Mary keeps a look out.

We grab the blankets and sheets and pillows off the beds, and

collect all the rugs we can, and towels, and laundry, and bath mats, and put them in a big pile, surrounded by chairs. And we even have to move some tables, and put the chairs on the tables, and we tie the whole thing up with a huge roll of ribbon. And the amazing thing is that we did this without my mum even noticing because she is on the phone.

"Dinner is ready!" calls my mum from the kitchen. Of course, Mrs Gobble Gracker is the first to arrive.

"Okay, now's your chance!" I tell Mr Nuggy. "Go and talk to her!"

From the fort, I can hear them in the kitchen.

"Good evening, Mrs Gobble Gracker."

"Is that you, Nuggy? *Nice dress.*"

"Thank you."

"I have an important message from Dory. You remember Dory – the baby you were coming for. She has agreed to go with you. Back to your cave. Forever."

"Great, because I had almost forgotten what I was doing here! Dory IS just what I wanted."

"But *after* dinner," he says.

"No problem," she says. "I'm starving."

Now that it's safe for me to leave my hiding spot, I come to the table for dinner. I sit next to Mrs Gobble Gracker because I don't want to miss the moment when she chokes on her poison soup and drops dead. Hee. Hee. Hee. Mr Nuggy and I make polite conversation.

"Do you like ice cream?" I ask Mrs Gobble Gracker.

"I can't think of anything more disgusting," she says.

"Do you have a mobile phone?" asks Mr Nuggy.

"No, but I really really want one," she says. "Can you get me one?"

"Umm ...?" says Mr Nuggy, looking unsure what to say next.

"Do you have a cat?" I interrupt.

"I ate my cat," she says. "It was an accident."

"Oh, then I suppose you aren't a vegetarian," I say.

"Yes," she says. "I would eat a vegetarian. Is that what we are having for dinner tonight?"

"We're having soup," says Mr Nuggy. "Just soup."

Everything is going smoothly until my dad comes home from work and sits on Mrs Gobble Gracker.

"It is?" says my dad, looking confused.

"You are sitting on Mrs Gobble Gracker!" I tell him. "Can you please move??"

"It's been a looooooooong day," says my mum to my dad.

At last everybody is at the table and sitting in their proper seat. Mr Nuggy serves the soup. Mrs Gobble Gracker picks up her spoon and tastes her soup.

119

"Delicious!!" says Mrs Gobble Gracker, spooning more into her mouth as it drips down her chin. The soup is a disaster. Nothing happens. No feathers in her ears. No yogurt-y eyeballs. This is the end of me.

Mr Nuggy whispers to me, "I'm so sorry. I must have forgotten an ingredient."

"Ouch!" screams Mrs Gobble Gracker. Mary bit her ankle under the table.

"Thanks for trying, Mary," I say. But nothing can save me now.

Mrs Gobble Gracker will probably bring me to her cave, I think, and put water in my cereal instead of milk and put me to bed too early, and not let me jump on her sofa, and she won't take me to the library, and she'll eat all of my sweets at Halloween, and she'll always forget to buy bubble bath, and she'll put soggy sandwiches in my lunchbox, and she'll say my nightgowns are too small and give them away to littler kids, and right

when it's time to light my birthday candles, she won't be able to find matches ... and ... and ... she might even cook me in a big pot!

"I'll miss you all," I tell my family. "I was such a great little girl, and now I'm going to be taken away forever."

"Bye!" says Violet.

"So long!" says Luke.

As I'm being carried away, out of the corner of my eye, I notice baby Cherry in her cradle in the living room. Suddenly, I realise I don't need anyone's help. I can save myself.

I wiggle out of Mrs Gobble Gracker's arms and run to pick up baby Cherry. I hold her up high so Mrs Gobble Gracker can get a good look.

She stares at Cherry. And she stares at me.
Then back to Cherry. Then back to me. I take a
deep breath and try to look very grown up.

"Humph!" she says, grabbing Cherry from
me. I open the door for her and just like that,

Mrs Gobble Gracker walks
out the door with *stupid old
baby Cherry*.

Then I hear screaming.

It's my mum. She found my giant fort.

CHAPTER 6
Bouncy Ball

It takes a really long time to clean up the fort because I keep forgetting that
I'm cleaning up.

"Rascal, bedtime!!!" calls
my mum. "Brush your teeth!"

As I brush my teeth, I say good night to Mr Nuggy. He has changed back into his normal clothes and is rushing home to see his wife.

That's when Violet bursts into the bathroom, crying. "I can't find Cherry anywhere!" she says. "And I've looked everywhere! She's gone!"

GULP

UH-OH. WHERE IS THAT DOLL?

"I'll be right back," I say.

I tiptoe downstairs and into the dark living room. *Oh! Where did I put Cherry?* I gave her to Mrs Gobble Gracker, of course. But what did I REALLY ACTUALLY do with her? Think, think, think, I tell myself. I check all the usual places ... the fridge, the toilet, the dishwasher, the rubbish, under the sofa,

in the sofa,

under the rug,

upstairs ...

In every drawer, under the beds, in the bath . . .

After looking everywhere, I found:

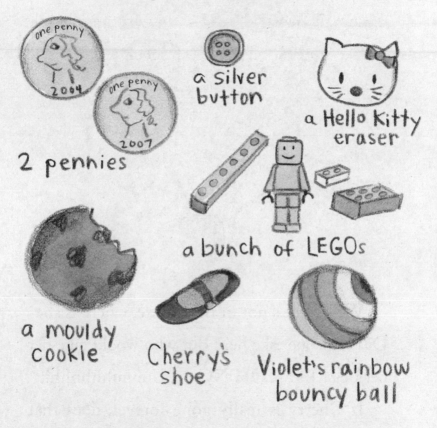

2 pennies

a silver button

a Hello Kitty eraser

a bunch of LEGOs

a mouldy cookie

Cherry's shoe

Violet's rainbow bouncy ball

But no Cherry. I put the bouncy ball in my pocket.

I'm so tired! I give up. Cherry is definitely not in this house.

Well if she's not in this house, where is she? Did someone take her? But who would take her besides Mrs . . . OH NO . . . Uuuuuhhhhh!!

If Cherry is really gone forever, does that mean Mrs Gobble Gracker IS REAL??

My dad hears my scream and comes running. "Why are you screaming like a maniac? You're going to wake up the whole neighborhood! Stop this right now and go to bed!"

"AAAAAAAAHHHHHHHHHHH!"

He drags me by the arm. "We've had enough of you for the day, Rascal. Everybody is fed up, got it?"

"AAAAAAAAHHHHHHHHHHH!"

"Stop screaming!!" screams my dad.

"SHE WAS REAL!!!!" I scream.

"Okay, calm down, she was real, whatever you say," says my dad, dragging me down the hallway to my room. "Just go to bed."

Even my dad said she's real!

HELP!

"I have to be brave," I say, clinging to him.

"No! You have to go to bed!" he says, dropping me on my bed.

"Stay. In. Bed!" he says, pointing his finger at me. Then he tucks me in tight. "Because it's not safe for you to come out!" he says as he shuts my door, and I think I hear him laugh a tiny bit.

I fake sleep for a few minutes and then when I'm sure my dad is back downstairs, I sneak out of my room. I'm going to tell Violet the truth. That Cherry is gone forever and *it's all my fault*. And even though I know she'll want to kill me, she doesn't have to even bother. Because Mrs Gobble Gracker is probably coming back for me.

I have an idea. After I tell her the bad news, I'll give Violet her old bouncy ball. That might make her feel *a little bit better*.

"Violet," I say quietly, clutching the bouncy ball tightly behind my back.

"What?" she says.

"There is something I have to tell you . . . um . . . I . . ."

But then, I don't believe what I see. My mouth drops open. *Is that Cherry?* Lying right there next to Violet? "How . . . how . . . how . . . did she get there?" I ask.

"Oh, Luke found her when he snuck outside to catch fireflies," says Violet. "I must've left her on the front step, but I don't know when."

"Oh," I say quietly. But inside my head, my thoughts are loud: OOOOOHHH!! The step!! Of course!! I threw her out the front door when Mrs Gobble Gracker was leaving!

"What did you want to tell me?" Violet asks.

"Oh yeah, that . . . well . . ." I say, climbing into her bed and tucking myself into her cozy warm covers.

"Well, Mrs Gobble Gracker isn't real after all," I say.

"I know. I'm the one who made her up, stupid."

"You did??? Oh yeah," I say. "Thanks, Violet, that was a fun game. But it got a little bit scary at the end."

I'm so happy that I get to stay home in this cozy little house with my family after all.

"Good night," I say to Violet.

"Good night," she says, giving me a little shove. "Now get into your own bed."

Before I get out of her bed,
I hide the rainbow bouncy ball
under Violet's pillow as
a secret little gift.

139

The next morning is Saturday and our parents are still asleep. Luke and Violet are playing with the bouncy ball that Violet found under her pillow.

They are laughing as the ball hits the ceiling and flies off the walls,

hitting them on

their heads.

"Let's bounce it on the stairs!" says Luke. On the stairs, they are laughing even harder.

I really wish I could play.

Suddenly it's quiet. I run upstairs to go look.

The bouncy ball . . . bounced into the toilet.
Luke and Violet stand over the toilet staring
down at the sunken ball.

"What should we do?" shrieks Violet.
"Are we in trouble?" asks Luke.

"We'll have to get it out," says Violet.

"How do we do that?" asks Luke.

And then they both turn around to find me behind them, watching. Smiling.

"Rascal will get it, won't you, Rascal?" says Violet, nodding her head yes.

Right away, I roll up my nightgown sleeve and I stick my arm deep into the bottom of the toilet.

Luke and Violet cringe and cover their eyes and make gagging noises.

"Here it is!" I say, holding up the bouncy ball, my arm dripping toilet water.

Violet squeezes practically the whole bottle of foamy soap on my arm and helps me wash my hands and the ball. "Thanks, Rascal," says Violet. "You saved the bouncy ball!" I am so happy. I am beaming! We all agree that we don't need to tell Mum and Dad.

All day, all I can think about is the bouncy ball. Every time I think about it, I feel so proud. "Remember when I saved the bouncy ball?" I ask Violet.

"Uh-huh," she says.

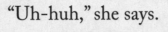

After dinner Luke says, "Rascal, close your eyes and open your hand."

My whole life I've always wanted someone to say this to me.

Before I even open my eyes, I know exactly what it is: it's the rainbow bouncy ball.

"You can *borrow* it, Rascal," Violet says. "It's not to keep!"

"Really?" I say. *"Really???"*

"Since you saved it," she says.

I hug Luke and Violet.

"Let's play!" says Luke.

"Yeah!" says Violet. "Bounce it!"

I try and think of the best bouncy ball game I can think of. I hold the bouncy ball very tightly, close my eyes, and concentrate.

All these pictures come
rushing into my brain
at once.

"Okay, I've got it! The ball is really a poison gum ball, and if it hits the ceiling, it explodes, and hot lava pours out of it, and we all melt. And when we melt, we turn back into cavemen, and Mrs Gobble Gracker lives in the cave next door and she . . ."

"No! Not Mrs Gobble Gracker *again*!" says Violet.

"Okay," I say, " but everything else?"

They agree. "Okay, everything else," they say.

My brother and my sister and I play bouncy ball. I run like a maniac to catch the ball, running into the walls, and screaming as it bonks me in the head. When the ball hits the ceiling we explode! I'm jumping up and down and making loud crashing sounds, the kind of sounds the earth makes when it blows up.

I leap onto Luke to protect myself from the hot lava. Hot lava is spilling all over the floor! It's bubbling everywhere! We jump on the sofa, and move the pillows around so that we have a secret cave.

Now we are
cave people!

Violet is the cave mummy, of course, and
Luke is the caveman daddy hunter, and guess
who gets to be the cave baby? ME! And I'm *the
cutest* little cave baby.

THE END